ROTTEN SCHOOL

LEARNING

GROWTH · PIZZA!

Shake, Rattle & HURL!

R.L. STINE

Illustrations by Trip Park

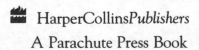

HarperCollins*Publishers*

A Parachute Press Book

For Cameron
–TP

First published in the USA by HarperCollins *Children's Books* 2006
First published in the UK by HarperCollins *Children's Books* 2006
HarperCollins *Children's Books* is an imprint of HarperCollins*Publishers* Ltd,
77-85 Fulham Palace Road, Hammersmith London W6 8JB

The HarperCollins *Children's Books* website address is
www.harpercollinschildrensbooks.co.uk

1 3 5 7 9 8 6 4 2

Shake, Rattle and Hurl
Copyright © 2006 by Parachute Publishing, L.L.C.
Cover copyright © 2006 by Parachute Publishing, L.L.C.

ISBN-10 0-00-721621-1
ISBN-13 978-0-00-721621-5

Printed and bound in England by
Clays Ltd, St Ives plc

— :CONTENTS:— —

Morning Announcements 11

1. How I Lost My Lunch 13

2. The Plopps 18

3. Bird Plop 24

4. Gassy Shows Off 30

5. The New Act Is BIG! 35

6. Heinie Trouble 39

7. Kidnapped! 43

8. Who's the Dummy? 48

9. Baloom Baloom 53

10. "Ow!" 62

11. The Greatest Rock Guitar Ever! ...70

12. A Star Is Born 74

13. Help from a Water Bottle 79

14. Not Nice in Nyce House 82

15. The Music Lover 85

16. Why I Sat on Chipmunk 92

17. Urrrrrrp 100

18. Urp Urp Urpurpurp 103

19. The Big Show 107

20. We Have a Winner and a Loser! 114

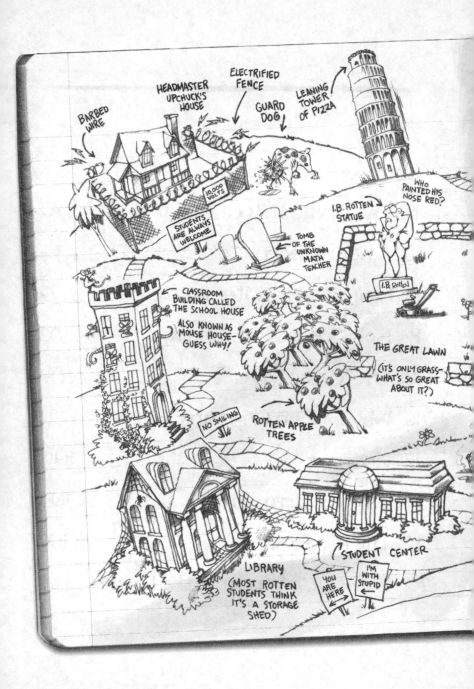

MORNING ANNOUNCEMENTS

Good morning, Rotten Students. This is Head-master Upchuck. I hope you're all ready for another Rotten day. Here are the Morning Announcements...

Congratulations to Eric Spindlebag, who won a national essay contest. The topic was: WHAT IT MEANS TO BE A CONCERNED CITIZEN OF OUR NATION. And Eric's essay was titled "What Do I Win?"

Buck Naykid, president of the Fifth-Grade Losers Club, makes this request: "Yes, we are losers. But we don't like to be called losers. We like to be called *winner-challenged*. Thank you."

Those students who insist on wearing superhero costumes to class: please hang your capes in your lockers. And make sure your tights fit properly so we don't have any more embarrassing problems like last Tuesday.

Nurse Hanley has an important reminder to all first graders: vaseline is *not* a food.

And here's a special dinner announcement: Chef Baloney announces that it's Endangered Species Night in the Dining Hall.

Chapter 1

HOW I LOST
MY LUNCH

"Yo! Looking way good today, dudes!" I said to my buddies Feenman and Crench.

"Thanks Bernie," Feenman said.

He had yellow stains on the front of his school blazer. That meant he had eggs for breakfast.

Crench's fly was open and the bottom of his school tie poked out.

They're both total slobs. But I like to encourage my guys. So I lie and tell them how good they look.

It's a *nice* lie, right?

They plopped their lunch trays down on the table.

13

"What are you eating, Bernie?" Feenman asked. He poked his nose into my plate.

"I'm on a health food kick," I said. "Pizza and French fries."

Down the table, our buddy Beast burped so hard he rocketed off his chair. When Beast burps, big chunks fly from his mouth and sail across the room.

If you don't duck in time, it can get pretty gross.

Beast climbed back up and began pawing food into his mouth with both hands. When he finished, he had chilli and spaghetti all over his face and stuck in his hair. For dessert he pulled stuff out of his hair and ate it.

I'm thinking of entering Beast in the school Talent Contest next week. His talent is making everyone *sick*!

My buddies and I have our own table in the Dining Hall – the Rotten House table. See, Rotten House is the name of the dorm we live in. Actually, it's a broken-down old house. But we love it.

We live on the third floor. Which is perfect for spitting on people down below. Of course, we'd *never* do such a rude thing. We'd never even *think* about it.

You probably go home every day after school. But we don't. The Rotten School is a boarding school. We live here.

I'm Bernie Bridges. Maybe you've heard of me. I mean, word *does* get around about guys who are smart and popular, and natural-born leaders.

I would *never* say that about myself, of course. But I've heard others say it about me.

I finished my pizza and admired my reflection in the empty plate. If only I weren't so modest! I could tell you what an awesome-looking dude I am.

I looked up and saw Beast emptying the salt and pepper shakers into his open mouth. Cool dude.

Lunch is always a fun time here in the Dining Hall. It's a huge room, with a cafeteria line at one end. And rows and rows of tables, enough for kids from all three dorms.

I started to get up to get another slice of pizza. But I stopped when I heard a sound at the front of the room.

A *honk*. And then a drumbeat. A *tweet*. Another *honk*.

I turned to the front and saw a band getting ready to play.

And that's when I nearly lost my lunch.

Chapter 2

THE PLOPPS

Which dorm do we Rotten House dudes hate the most?

Nyce House.

And there, at the front of the Dining Hall, stood the Nyce House Band, getting ready to play.

I saw my archenemy, that spoilt rich kid Sherman Oaks. Sherman has no talent. He's *too rich* to bother with talent.

So he always stands to the side and shakes a tambourine. Sometimes, he hires a kid to shake the tambourine for him!

The star of the band is Sherman's good buddy Wes Updood. Wes is maybe the best saxophone player in the universe. Even counting planets that haven't been discovered yet. He's *that* good. He's also the coolest dude in school. Disgusting, right? I watched Sherman Oaks step up to a microphone. "Hello, dudes and dudettes," he boomed, tossing back his perfect blond hair. "You all know me. The one-and-only Sherman Oaks. My Nyce House Band came to play for you today.

19

No need to applaud. We know we're *way* fabulous!"

I stuck my finger down my throat and made a gagging noise.

Wes stepped up beside Sherman, carrying his saxophone. "Jack of diamonds, everyone!" he said. "Jack of diamonds, man. Silver dollars – no change!"

I told you Wes is the coolest guy in school. He's so totally cool, no one ever knows what he's *talking* about!

"Silver dollars!" Wes repeated, pumping his fist in the air. "Pudding for everyone! Blue skies, people!"

20

Huh? I wish I was cool enough to understand that.

Wes raised his saxophone to his mouth, and the band started to play. Kids all over the Dining Hall started to clap as music poured from Wes's sax.

His hands moved frantically over the horn. He swung it from side to side. He leaned way back and let the notes float up to the rafters. Then he ducked low and the sounds came out like an animal growl.

As the other players kept the beat, Wes made his saxophone sing and honk and wail and cry.

I felt sick. I hated the grin on Sherman's face as he shook his tambourine, his eyes closed.

I glanced around the big room. Kids were *loving* it. My eyes stopped at the girls' table near the band. I saw April-May June rocking and bopping to the music.

April-May June, *my* girlfriend – only she doesn't know it yet. She was swaying from side to side, clapping her hands – really into it.

Oh, sick.

I had to look away. I turned to Feenman and Crench. Crench was slapping his hands to the rhythm, slapping them on Feenman's head.

"Stop it," I said. "What is the big deal here?" I had to shout over the music.

"Wes is awesome!" Feenman said, shaking his head in time to the music.

"Give me a break." I groaned. "What's so hard about playing a saxophone? You blow into it and move your fingers around. That's all there is to it."

"Wes Updood is gonna win the Talent Contest again this year," Feenman said.

I rolled my gorgeous brown eyes. "So what?"

Feenman leaned closer. "Know what the prize is? Two tickets to see The Plopps concert. *And* you get to meet them backstage."

"The Plopps?" I started to choke. Feenman had to pound me on the back. "The P-p-plopps?" I gasped.

My heart pounded. My eyeballs started rolling around in my head.

"The Plopps?" I cried, leaping to my feet. "They're my favourite band! I've downloaded every song they ever did!"

"Easy Bernie, easy," Crench said, pulling me back into my seat.

But I couldn't calm down. "The Plopps! The Plopps!" I cried. "Have you heard their greatest hits CD? *Plopping Across America?*"

I realised I was drooling.

Crench wiped my chin for me with his blazer sleeve. "Yeah," he said. "Those two Plopp sisters are *hot.*"

"I can't believe Wes Updood is gonna meet them," Feenman said. "And he'll probably take his best buddy, Sherman Oaks, to the concert with him."

"No way!" I said. I jumped to my feet again. "Rotten House has *got* to win the Talent Contest this year! I'm going to that Plopps concert. No one can stop me!"

Chapter 3

BIRD PLOP

Famous last words, right?

"Bernie, we can't win the Talent Contest," Feenman said, shaking his head.

"Yeah. We've got one little problem," Crench said.

"Problem? What problem?" I asked.

They both answered together: "We don't have any TALENT!"

I felt sick. I ate three more slices of pizza, but they didn't go down well.

I sat at the table, watching the Nyce House Band, thinking hard. Thinking about the awesome Plopp

sisters. I had to meet them. I *had* to win the contest.

Wes Updood jumped up on a table. He leaned way back, blowing his heart out, rocking the room. He played so hard and loud, his face turned bright red, his ears popped out and his hair stood straight up on end.

All the kids in the Dining Hall crowded around the table. They were clapping and shouting and dancing and rocking to the music.

Big deal, I thought.

So he's talented. It takes more than *talent* to win a talent show.

After lunch, I caught up with April-May June on the Great Lawn. It was a warm, sunny day. Butterflies fluttered over the grass. Birds twittered in the branches of the rotten apple trees.

"Hey, whussup?" I said to April-May. "I like what you did with your hair. Is that a new hair clip or something?"

"I have bird plop in my hair," she said. "I should never walk under the apple trees. I'm hurrying to my room to wash it out."

April-May always acts like she's in a hurry whenever I see her. That's because she doesn't know she's my girlfriend yet.

I had to jog to keep up with her. "April-May, can I ask you an important question?" I said.

"No," she answered. She started to run faster.

"Would you like to come see The Plopps concert with me?" I shouted after her.

"I'm going to the concert with Wes Updood," she said. "After he wins the Talent Contest."

I tackled her around the waist to slow her down. "What if Wes doesn't win?" I said.

She tossed back her head and laughed for about five minutes. "Bernie, did you just hear Wes play? He was *awesome*! He's the most talented kid in the whole school!"

I rolled my eyes. "April-May, there's more to life than being the most talented," I said. "What about good looks?"

I pulled off my glasses and flashed her my best smile. When I smile I have two adorable dimples in my cheeks. It's my best feature. It takes a heart of stone to ignore them.

"Take your good looks for a long walk, Bernie," April-May said.

She took off, running full speed towards the girls' dorm. Her blond hair flew behind her. The big hunk of bird plop glowed in the sunlight.

"Does that mean you'll go with me?" I shouted.

She made a rude spitting noise.

I took that for a *maybe*.

I walked off, muttering to myself. I talk to myself a lot. Who *else* understands pure genius?

"You'll see," I said. "You'll change your mind, April-May. I'm gonna win that contest. You'll see. I've got a plan..."

Chapter 4

GASSY SHOWS OFF

After dinner I hurried back to Rotten House and gathered my buddies in my room.

Feenman, Crench and Belzer are crammed into the tiny room across the hall from me. It used to be a closet. I have my own room about five times as big.

They insisted I take it. They wanted me to have my own room. They knew I need a lot of space for scheming and thinking and planning. And I needed space to hang my favourite poster – the life-size poster of ME!

Feenman and Crench were fighting over a bag of

crisps. They kept snatching the bag out of each other's hands – until the bag tore open and the crisps all fell to the floor.

Gassy, my big, beautiful bulldog, dived on the chips and snuffled them all up in less than ten seconds, and then licked all the salt off the floor.

Can you guess how Gassy got his name?

I turned to my friend Belzer. "Did you walk Gassy tonight?"

Belzer flashed me his crooked grin. He had taken off his school blazer. He was wearing a T-shirt with big red letters that said: PARDON MY FRENCH.

I don't know where he finds these lame T-shirts.

"I walked Gassy," Belzer said. "Then I fed him."

"Did you taste his food first to make sure it was warm enough?" I asked.

Belzer nodded. "I ate a few spoonfuls out of the can."

Good kid, Belzer. It took a long time to train him. But it was worth it.

My three friends dropped down on the edge of my bed. "Don't wrinkle the bedspread," I said. "It's pure silk."

I pulled Gassy into the centre of the room. "OK, quiet everyone. Quiet. I'm gonna show you the *killer* act that's gonna win the Talent Contest."

I started to feel excited. I knew I had something BIG.

"What's your act, Bernie?" Crench asked. "Card tricks or something?"

"Crench," I answered, "why would I do card tricks when I have Gassy the Great here?"

I pulled the fat bulldog to his feet. He plopped on his stomach again.

"Belzer, hold him up," I said. "You know he doesn't like to stand up on his own."

Belzer grabbed Gassy around the belly and hoisted him to his feet.

"Now watch carefully, dudes," I said. "An amazing trick. I taught Gassy how to count to one!"

"Huh?" Crench said, scratching his hair. "Bernie, *one* isn't very high."

"For a dog?" I cried. "For a dog, it's like counting to a *million*! It's taken me all week to get him to count to one. But watch. It's brilliant. It can't lose."

Belzer held the dog up. I stared Gassy in the eye.

"Go ahead, boy," I said. "Start counting!"

Gassy didn't move. Then we heard a long, loud

BRRRAAAP.

"Ohhhh!" Belzer let out a groan and let go of the dog. "He stinks! Oh man, he STINKS! Air! Air! I need AIR!"

Feenman and Crench held their noses.

"Bernie, your act STINKS!" Feenman said.

"But that's ONE!" I exclaimed. "Don't you see? That's how he counts to one!"

BRRRAAAP.

Another loud noise from the fat bulldog.

"Isn't he *brilliant?*" I asked. "Isn't he a *genius?* He just counted to *two!*"

"I can't breathe. Air! Air!" Belzer moaned.

"Go stick your head out of the window," I said.

But there was no room. Feenman and Crench already had their heads out of the window.

"OK. OK. Forget Gassy," I said. "I've got a better act. This act will *kill*! It can't lose."

Chapter 5

THE NEW ACT
IS BIG!

"Dudes, check this out," I said. I pulled Feenman and Crench back to the bed. "Sit down. Watch this."

"You've got another act, Bernie?" Belzer asked.

I nodded. "Bernie B *always* has another act!" I said. "I'm gonna win the Talent Contest for Rotten House. Have I ever let you guys down?"

"Never!" they all cried at once.

"Am I always there for you guys?" I asked.

"Always!" they all cried at once.

"Who convinced Mrs Heinie to give extra credit if we stay in our seats for a whole class?" Belzer asked.

"Bernie did!" Feenman and Crench cheered.

"And who convinced Chef Baloney that Gummi Worms are an important part of a healthy breakfast?" Belzer cried.

"Bernie did!" Feenman and Crench chanted.

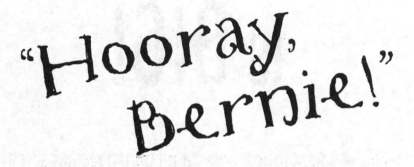

"Hooray, Bernie!"

Belzer pumped his fists in the air. "And who convinced Headmaster Upchuck to put SpongeBob SquarePants on the Rotten School Honour Roll of Famous Living Americans?"

"Actually, Billy the Brain did that," I said.

Billy lives downstairs. He's the brainiest kid in school. But for some reason he thinks SpongeBob SquarePants is *real*.

Anyway, we all cheered and slapped high fives, and did the secret Rotten House Handshake.

"OK, simmer down guys," I said. "I want to show you this new act. This one can't lose. I'm going to do impressions of all our teachers. The judges will go crazy for this."

Feenman squinted at me. "Impressions? What kind of impressions?" he asked.

"Watch," I said.

I took off my glasses and pulled on a pair of inch-thick glasses. Then I turned to Belzer. "Take the two pillows off my bed," I said. "Stuff them down the back of my jeans."

Feenman and Crench gaped at me as if I were nuts. But Belzer is trained never to ask questions. He took the pillows and jammed them down the back of my jeans.

"OK, who am I?" I said.

They stared at me.

"I'm Mrs Heinie," I said. "Get it?" I strutted around the room, bent forwards staring through the thick eyeglasses with my huge butt sticking out behind me.

"Get it? Look at the size of this butt! I'm Mrs Heinie! Brilliant?"

"Uh… not too brilliant," Crench muttered. He and Feenman were staring over my shoulder.

I turned to the open door.

Guess who was standing there.

You got it.

Mrs Heinie.

Chapter 6

HEINIE TROUBLE

I squinted through my thick eyeglasses – and saw Mrs Heinie squinting back at me through *her* thick eyeglasses.

Uh-oh. Double uh-oh.

Was she smiling? No. I wouldn't describe the look on her face as a smile. I'd describe it as the look people have in a horror movie when they see the ugly, evil, man-eating monster for the first time.

Behind the glasses her eyes were bulging like tennis balls, and her mouth had dropped open to her knees.

Mrs Heinie is our teacher and our dorm mother. And we all think she's terrific. She's not a kind person, but she's very fair.

She has a job to do as dorm mother. And that job is to keep us from being us. In other words, she has to make sure that we don't have *too much* fun.

It's a tough job. And despite the fact that she's a little short-sighted and a little bent over, she's a tough woman.

And now here she was in the doorway to my room, watching me strut around, doing my two-pillow impression of her.

Most kids would fall to the floor and start to cry and plead insanity.

But not Bernie Bridges. Do you think I can't talk my way out of anything?

"Yo, Mrs Heinie," I greeted her with my most

adorable, dimpled smile. "Would you like to join our game?"

She made a choking sound. Her bulging eyes were locked on my huge butt. "Game?"

"Yes, we're having such awesome fun," I said, keeping the dimples flashing. "We're playing Pillow Search. It's a totally popular game. Everyone in the dorm is playing it."

Mrs Heinie made another choking sound. "Popular?" she said.

"You're looking lovely tonight, Mrs H," I said. "I see you're dressed up. Are you going to a fancy party? I *know* you. I know you have a secret party life we boys don't know about."

"Bernie, I'm wearing my bathrobe," she said. She frowned at me. "Let's get back to the game."

"Oh, yes," I said. "The game. See? The rules are pretty simple. We take turns hiding the pillow. Then everyone tackles the guy with the pillow."

I turned to Feenman, Crench and Belzer. "OK. Tackle me, guys. Go ahead. Tackle me. Show Mrs H how the game works.

My three friends didn't move. They sat hunched on the bed, paralysed, staring at me with their mouths hanging open.

"Ha-ha." I laughed. "They're a little shy. But it's a great game. We play it all the time."

Mrs Heinie didn't move. She just stared at me, frowning, her face wrinkled up tight like a very pale prune.

"Uh… are you buying this story?" I asked.

She rolled her eyes. "What do *you* think?"

I swallowed noisily. "So… I'm in major trouble?"

She nodded. "Yes. Major trouble." She spun around and started to leave. But then she stuck her head back in the door. "You know, Bernie," she said, "*one* pillow would have been enough!"

Chapter 7

KIDNAPPED!

We waited for Mrs Heinie to go up the stairs to her apartment in the attic. Then we all fell on the floor laughing. Feenman pulled the pillows from my trousers, and we had a big pillow fight. Just letting off some steam.

Finally, I got everyone quiet. "Dudes, we still need an act for the Talent Contest," I said. "Hey, I've got another idea."

I pulled a bunch of toilet paper rolls out from a desk drawer. I'm not sure why I was saving them. I knew they'd come in handy one day.

I handed each guy a toilet paper roll. "We'll hum into them," I said. "We'll totally rock. Come on, dudes. Let's work up some awesome harmony. We'll play better than Wes's band."

I hummed a rock riff into my toilet paper roll.

Feenman made a disgusted face. "Sorry, Big B," he said. "That idea totally *wipes*."

I think he was making a joke. But he was right.

I slapped myself on the forehead. "Come on, Bernie. Think. *Think* of something!"

I *had* to come up with an act to beat Wes Updood.

"Hey, I'm going out, guys," I said. "I'm gonna take a walk. Sometimes fresh air helps me think."

They didn't hear me. They were singing into their toilet paper rolls at the top of their lungs.

I hurried downstairs and stepped out through the front door. It was a clear, warm night. An owl hooted high in a nearby tree.

I took a deep breath and inhaled the strong aroma from the rotten apple trees on the Great Lawn. Mmmmm. Nothing like that smell to wake up your brain.

Sometimes I head over to Pooper's Pond to stare at the water and think. Don't ask me how the pond got that name. No one seems to know.

I turned and started to follow the narrow path to the pond.

And who was the first kid I ran into? Wes Updood. Carrying his saxophone case at his side.

"What's up, Wes?" I said. "You going to band practice?"

"Marshmallow Fluff, dude," he replied. "It's like Custer's Last Stand. Know what I mean? Extra creamy, with half the carbs."

"Cool," I said. I kept walking.

I was almost to the pond when strong hands grabbed me around the waist and spun me around.

I stared into the chunky, panting face of *Jennifer Ecch!*

I call her Nightmare Girl. That's because she's twice as big as I am, twice as strong – and totally in love with me.

A nightmare.

Do you know how *embarrassing* it is to be in fourth grade and have a girl who follows you around making loud smoochy noises and calling you "Honey Lips" and "Butter Cakes"?

It totally *wipes*!

"Hurry," she whispered. She picked me up off the ground.

"No!" I cried. "Jennifer – don't touch me. I have a flesh-eating disease. You don't want to catch it. It'll eat *your* flesh, too!"

She ignored me. She hoisted me over her broad shoulders and started to jog across the grass.

"Where are you taking me?" I cried, bouncing on her shoulder. "What are you doing?"

"Shhh. Quiet, Honey Face," she said. "Come with me. We're gonna win the Talent Contest!"

Chapter 8

WHO'S THE DUMMY?

Jennifer carried me into the girls' dorm. I heard girls giggling as she trotted down the front hall.

Finally, she set me down in the Commons Room. Every dorm has a Commons Room. It's like a big living room for everyone living in the dorm. You know. Couches and big armchairs, a TV, a game table.

I glanced around. We were the only ones there.

"Jennifer, I have to get back to my dorm," I said, glancing at the clock over the mantel. "I'm already in trouble with Mrs Heinie. I can't—"

"Shut up, Sweet Breath," she said. She grabbed

my arm and yanked me across the room to a big red armchair. "I heard you love The Plopps. Do you want to go to their concert or not?"

"Of course, I do," I said. "But—"

"Well, I know how we can do it," Jennifer said. She blew the hair from her eyes. She does that all the time. It's a habit, I guess. But I really hate it when she blows the hair from *my* eyes!

"How can we win the Talent Contest?" I asked. "Do you have a secret talent?"

"Of *course!*" she answered.

This was starting to get interesting.

I know. I know. I usually do *anything* to keep away from Jennifer Ecch. I once jumped in Pooper's Pond and stayed underwater for three minutes to keep her from seeing me.

That's pretty gross – right?

But tonight I was desperate. Desperate to beat Sherman and Wes and Nyce House. And desperate to see The Plopps.

"What's your talent?" I asked The Ecch. "Do you *eat* an entire car?"

"Don't be stupid, Sweet Ears," Jennifer said. "I'm

a great ventriloquist. I can throw my voice."

I stared at her. First at her blue eye, then at her brown eye. "No joke?"

"I just threw my voice," she said. "Could you hear it?"

"No," I replied.

"That's because I threw it really far," she said. She blew the hair out of her eyes again. "Listen, Bernie, we can do an awesome act together and win the big prize."

"I don't get it," I said. "Why do you need me?"

"I don't have a dummy," Jennifer said. "I can't do a ventriloquist act without a dummy. So… you're *it*."

"Huh? No *way*!" I cried.

She grinned. "You *love* the idea – don't you! I can tell. It'll be a *riot*, Honey Knees."

"PLEEEASE don't call me Honey Knees!" I begged.

"How can we lose?" Jennifer said.

She grabbed me and pulled me down on to her lap on the chair.

"This act is gonna be way wicked," she said.

"There's never been a ventriloquist act like this."
She slid her arms around my waist. I felt her hot
breath on the back of my neck.

"OK," I said. "Let's start."

Hello,
I just LOVE
Honey Face!

I waited for her to throw her voice. Or tell a joke. Or ask me a question or something.

I waited. And waited.

And waited.

"Uh… Jennifer?" I said.

She grabbed my hand. Squeezed it in both of hers. And started planting smoochy kisses all over it.

"Uh… Jen," I said quietly, "you're not a ventriloquist – are you?"

Smooch. Smooch. Smooch.

My hand was sopping wet.

"Uh… well… no." She finally answered my question.

"You can't throw your voice – can you?" I asked.

Smooch smooch.

"No, Lovey Chin. Actually, I can't."

I sighed. "And this was just an excuse to get me to sit in your lap, *wasn't* it!" I exclaimed.

"Yes," she said.

Chapter 9

BABOOM BABOOM

The next afternoon I ran into Sherman Oaks outside the School House, our classroom building. He flashed me his perfect, 65-toothed smile. "Guess where I'm coming from, Bernie."

"Having your head bronzed?" I said.

"No. Headmaster Upchuck's office. We were practising." Sherman smiled again, an even brighter smile. So bright, I had to shield my eyes.

"I envy you," I said. "Headmaster Upchuck is a man among men. He's a man I look up to. Well, yes, he's only three feet tall. I guess I can't really look *up* to him. But what does that matter? The man is a GIANT. He—"

Sherman rolled his eyes. "Bernie, aren't you going to ask me what we were practising in his office?"

"OK," I said. "What were you practising?"

"Him handing me the First Prize trophy for winning the Talent Contest," Sherman said.

"Excuse me?" *Gulp.* I swallowed my bubble gum. "You— you—"

"The Headmaster likes to get it right," Sherman said. "You know. When he comes on stage at the end to give the trophy to the winner? He wants the handoff to be smooth. So he and I practised it for about an hour."

I took a deep breath. "But he handed it to the wrong guy, Sherman," I said.

"Because you're not going to win. I am!"

Sherman tossed back his head, opened his mouth wide and laughed for about ten minutes. He laughed until he got the hiccups.

Then, wiping the tears from his eyes, he took my arm. "Come here, Bernie – *HIC*. Let me show you – *HIC* – one more reason you're not going to win."

He dragged me into Nyce House, his dorm. I instantly started to shake and sweat. The place gives me the deep creeps. It's clean and neat and quiet.

Who would *live* in a place like that?

As we passed the front hall I saw the dorm parents, Sam and Janet Pocketlint. They wore matching school uniforms and carried matching dust mops.

They were dusting everything in sight.

Gross.

Sherman pulled me into his room. I nearly gagged. The bed was made!

He had a furry, white sheepskin bedspread, and a sheepskin rug covered his floor. He had a wide-screen TV on his dresser. A music system with huge floor speakers that nearly reached the ceiling. On the wall above his bed he had a big green-and-black poster of a *dollar sign*.

"Check this out," Sherman said. He dragged me to a large keyboard standing against the wall. "This is my new digital drum machine," he said.

I was still shaking and sweating. But I pulled myself together. "Very nice, Shermy," I said, slapping him on the back. "And what do you plan to do with it? Annoy your neighbors?"

"No," he said. "My parents bought it for me so I can play drums in Wes Updood's band." He glanced at the big dollar sign on the wall. "It cost five thousand dollars. But my parents really want to buy my love."

"But you don't know *how* to play drums," I said.

He sneered. "What does *that* matter?" He clicked the power switch on. A soft rhythm started. He turned up the volume.

"See? You pick any rhythm," he said. "Then you pick a speed. Here."

He turned a knob. I heard

BOOM BABOOM
BABOOM BOOM.

"There it goes," Sherman said. "Sweet, huh? It's perfect for the band's first number."

"But what do *you* do?" I asked.

Sherman squinted at me. "Me? I don't do anything. It's all digital. It plays itself. I'm too rich. Why work up a sweat?"

"Can I try it?" I asked. "Hmm. Let me see…"

I grabbed the volume knob. "Is this the rhythm knob?"

I turned it up all the way.

BOOM
BABOOOM
BABOOOOM
BOOOOM

A deafening roar blasted from the machine. Two windows broke.

Sherman covered his ears. "Turn it down!" he shrieked. "Bernie! The volume! Turn it DOWN!"

I pretended I couldn't find the volume. "Which knob is it?" I screamed. "Is it this one? No. How about this one? No. Sorry, Sherman. I'm just not good with these digital things."

I pulled the volume knob off and held it in the air. "Is this it? I think it's broken."

BOOM
BABOOOM
BABOOOOM
BOOOOM

The walls were shaking. I saw a big crack split the ceiling. The sheepskins were jumping as if they had come alive!

Sherman fell to his knees, covering his ears, wailing in agony.

It was *way* painful.

I took off running. The throbbing, electronic drumbeats were shaking the whole house.

I was nearly out of the front door. But I stopped at the entrance to the Commons Room.

"Whoa." I saw April-May June. She was sitting on a couch beside Wes Updood.

What's up with that?

He was playing his saxophone. Showing off. He was making it honk like a duck and making it do gross, rude noises.

And April-May was slapping her knees, tossing back her blond hair, laughing her head off. She thought Wes was a riot.

"She doesn't *really* like Wes Updood," I growled to myself. "She likes *me*. She just doesn't know it yet. When Rotten House wins the Talent Contest, she'll be *begging* me to take her to The Plopps concert."

The honking stopped. Wes saw me in the

doorway. He waved.

"Instant pancakes, dude!" he called to me. "Yo, Bernie – instant pancakes, man! Nothing but the best. Know what I'm saying?"

"Yeah. Instant pancakes," I replied. And I hurried out of the door.

Chapter 10

"OW!"

Belzer, Feenman and Crench jammed into my room after dinner. They seemed very excited. All three of them were talking at once.

"We've got it, Big B!"

"We're gonna win."

"We've got the act. We've got it!"

"Well, it's about time," I said, jumping up from my computer. "I knew my guys would come through. You found a fabulously talented dude hiding in the dorm?"

"Not exactly," Belzer said.

"Belzer, did you have spinach at dinner?" I asked.

"Well, yeah," he replied. "How'd you know?"

"You've got big, green globs of spinach stuck to your braces."

"No problem, Big B," he said. "It always dissolves in two or three days."

Feenman pulled me away from Belzer. "Bernie, forget the spinach. You've gotta see our act. We're the *best!*"

"*Your* act?" I took a few steps back. "You three? What kind of an act? Guess what, guys? Eating a double cheeseburger without chewing is *not* a talent!"

"We've got a better act than that," Crench said. "You ever see those old comedics on TV? The black-and-white ones with those three nutty weirdos?"

"*The Three Stooges?*" I asked.

"Yeah," Crench said. "Those dudes who are always slapping each other, hitting and kicking, and poking each other's eyes out. They're cool, right?"

"So guess what we decided to do?" Belzer said, picking long strings of spinach from between his teeth.

I stared at my friends. I counted them. One, two, three. "You guys are going to do a *Three Stooges* act?" I said.

"Wow. How did you guess that?" Feenman asked.

"Check out the act, Bernie," Crench said. "We're not just funny. We're a *riot*. The judges at the Talent Contest will fall down. Really. Forget Wes Updood. We've got it won! Watch!"

Belzer disappeared into their room across the hall for a minute. He came back carrying a baseball bat. "OK. Ready, guys?" he asked.

"Here goes, Bernie," Crench said. "Get ready to laugh."

"I'm ready," I said. "Go ahead. Be funny."

They started their act.

"Hey, you—!" Feenman said to Crench.

"Don't say *hey*," Crench said.

"I'll say whatever I want," Feenman said. He slapped Crench's face.

Crench raised his hand to slap Feenman. Feenman ducked and Crench slapped Belzer instead.

"Hey! What did I do?" Belzer shouted. He punched Crench in the stomach.

Crench doubled over.

"$Owwww$."

Feenman poked Belzer in the eyes.

"$Owwwwww$."

Belzer punched Feenman in the chest. The punches and slaps flew. Crench slammed the baseball bat into Belzer's stomach.

"$Owwww!$"

"That really hurt!"

"Ohhhhh. I'm bleeding. I'm bleeding!"

"You poked my eyes out! I can't see! You poked my eyes out!"

"$Owwwwww$."

"Help me!"

"It hurts! It hurts!"

"My head hurts! I can't see!"

I started to laugh. "Good work, dudes!" I said.

"That's a riot! That's totally funny!" I laughed some more.

They were rolling on the floor, moaning, holding their heads and their stomachs.

"Not… funny," Belzer groaned. "Bernie, we're in pain. We're not faking it. We really *destroyed* each other!"

"I think I got a concussion," Feenman wailed.

"My… head," Crench moaned. "It feels like my skull is fractured!"

I stopped laughing. "Guys, guys – get up!" I tried to pull them to their feet. But they were doubled over in pain.

"You know," I told them, "I don't think the Three Stooges really injured themselves in those old movies. I think they kinda *faked* it."

"You… think… so?" Crench groaned, holding his stomach.

"They *faked* it?" Feenman said, hands covering his eyes.

"Yeah. They didn't really punch each other and poke out each other's eyes. They just pretended," I said. "You guys have to work on the *pretending* part.

I think you need more practice."

Crench groaned. "Why didn't someone *tell* us they faked it?"

They couldn't stand up. So I rolled them out into the hall. Then I closed my bedroom door.

"What am I gonna do?" I asked myself. "The rehearsal for the Talent Contest is tomorrow night. And I've got nothing. *Nothing*."

I have to search the dorm from top to bottom, I decided.

There *has* to be someone in Rotten House with some talent.

I decided to search every room on every floor.

I opened my door and walked into the hall. I had to step over Belzer, Feenman and Crench to get to the stairs.

I made my way down to the second floor – and stopped.

I froze. My ears stood up on end. My heart started to pound.

"Whoa!" I cried. "What is THAT?!"

Chapter 11

THE GREATEST ROCK GUITAR EVER!

I grabbed the banister and listened. Where was that music coming from?

I held my breath. The music was *awesome*. Rock-and-roll guitar. Wailing, soaring, *rocking* sounds.

It's a CD, I decided.

One of the guys is playing a CD of a totally great guitar player.

But no. The music stopped for a moment. Then started up again, playing the same song, only in a different rhythm.

My fingers were snapping in time to the beat. I

didn't even realise it. My legs were moving. My knees were dipping. I was DANCING!

I couldn't help it. The guitar totally *kicked*!

I'd never heard rock-and-roll guitar like that *in my life*!

Now I gripped the banister with both hands. Sweat poured down my broad, handsome forehead. My heart was doing a rock-and-roll beat in my chest!

"Someone in this dorm can play *awesome* guitar," I told myself. "I've gotta find him. I *need* him! He's gonna win the Talent Contest for me!"

I jumped off the stairs and into the second-floor hallway. Down at the far end of the hall, a bunch of second graders were laughing and shrieking, pulling down each other's jeans. They have de-trousering contests just about every night.

They're *so* immature.

I grabbed the doorknob on the first door I came to and pushed open the door.

My friend Nosebleed was sitting at his desk, staring at a blank sheet of paper. "What are you doing?" I asked him.

He shrugged. "I don't know. Just staring. It helps me think."

"Think about what?" I asked.

He shrugged again. "I don't know."

"Were you playing that rock guitar?" I asked him.

He shook his head. "No way. I can't play a musical instrument. It gives me a nosebleed."

I slammed his door and hurried to the next room. Down the hall, the second graders were all dancing around in their underpants.

I pulled open the next door and saw Billy the Brain sitting at his desk.

Billy has a solid C-minus average. Incredible, right? He's the smartest kid in school.

"Who's there?" Billy called. He was sitting at his desk, doing his homework *blindfolded*.

"It's me. Bernie," I said. "Why are you blindfolded?"

"To make it harder," Billy said. "I read all of my textbooks blindfolded so I won't have an unfair advantage over the rest of you dumber guys."

What a brain!

"Were you just playing guitar?" I asked him.

"I don't play guitar," Billy said. "But sometimes I

play the piano blindfolded."

I *told* you he's brilliant!

I slammed his door and hurried down the hall. I took the stairs two at a time to the second floor.

I could hear the rock guitar even louder now. Twanging, swooping, *rocking*!

Where was it coming from?

I stopped outside Chipmunk's door. The music grew louder. Was it possible?

Chipmunk is the shyest kid in school. He's so shy, he inhales when he *burps*!

I like to help my guys. I've been working with Chipmunk. Trying to get him over his shyness. But so far, even Bernie B has failed.

"It can't be Chipmunk playing this awesome guitar," I muttered. "No way."

I pressed my ear to the door.

Yes! The music was definitely coming from inside.

I pushed open the door. "Chipmunk?" I called. "Is that *you* playing?"

My eyes searched the room. No one there.

"Chipmunk?"

Where *was* he?

Chapter 12

A Star Is Born

I stepped into the room. The rocking guitar swooped and soared and twanged. "Chipmunk?" I called.

I followed my ears – to the closet. I pulled open the closet door. "Yo – Chipmunk!" I cried.

He sat on a pile of dirty shirts and pants, a shiny new guitar in his hands.

"Hi, Bernie," he said, blushing. He blushes whenever he talks.

I stared down at him. "Chipmunk – were you playing that *awesome* guitar?"

He blushed some more. "I'll stop if you want me to," he said, lowering his eyes.

"Huh? Stop?" I cried. "You don't understand. You've gotta keep playing."

"I—I do?" he stammered, gripping the guitar in both hands.

"Why are you in the closet?" I asked.

"I don't want to bother anyone," Chipmunk replied, his eyes still down.

"Don't you realise?" I shouted. "Don't you realize you play the wickedest rock guitar I ever heard!"

He shrugged. "I practise a lot," he whispered. "I think I'm getting better." He blushed again.

I grabbed him with both hands and tugged him out of the closet. "You're gonna be a winner, Chipmunk!"

He blinked. "I am?"

"You want to get over your shyness, right? Right," I answered for him. "Well this is your big chance."

He started to shake. "What do I have to do?" he asked in a trembling voice.

I slapped him on the back. "Play guitar, that's all," I said. "You're going to play at the Talent Contest rehearsal tomorrow after school. You're gonna be our talent."

"I—I am?" He squeezed his guitar so hard, his hands turned red.

"Chipmunk, you *rock*, dude! No way you can lose," I told him. "Everyone will fall on the floor and beg you to play some more. You'll kill! *Kill!*"

Chipmunk swallowed a few times. His big Adam's apple slid up and down. "But— but—" he sputtered.

"No buts," I said. "You've already *won*." I started for the door. "I'm gonna bring all the guys downstairs to hear you play."

"But, but— Bernie—"

"Don't move," I said. "The guys have got to hear you *rock out!*"

I ran upstairs. No. Actually, I *flew* upstairs.

I rounded up everyone – Feenman, Crench, Belzer, Nosebleed, Billy the Brain, Farley Mopes, Beast and a bunch of other dudes. I led them all down to Chipmunk's room.

"You're gonna fall to the ground!" I told them. "You're gonna rock till you drop! This is totally amazing!"

I pushed open Chipmunk's door, and we all rushed inside.

"Chipmunk?"

He was gone.

Chapter 13

HELP FROM A WATER BOTTLE

I glanced all around. "Where is he? Where is he? He can't have gone far! Find him!"

We scrambled all over the room. I pulled open the closet door. No sign of him. I tossed out the pile of dirty clothes. No. He wasn't hiding under them.

We looked everywhere – even in the dresser drawers.

Finally, Feenman found him hiding under the bed. "What are you doing under there?" he asked.

"Uh… I do this sometimes," Chipmunk replied. "It's, um, nice under here."

"It's nice out here, too," I said. "Come out and play."

Feenman and Crench grabbed his arms and legs and pulled him out. I handed him his guitar. "Play," I said. "The guys can't wait to hear you."

He swallowed a few more times.

"Play," I said. "Rock-and-roll forever – right?"

"I guess," he muttered. He carried his guitar into the closet and closed the door behind him.

"Bernie," Feenman said, "what's with the closet?"

"Just shut up and listen," I said. "The dude is an artist. He can play wherever he wants."

A few seconds later, Chipmunk started playing. The guitar totally *rocked*!

Chipmunk's playing had a pounding beat. It was bluesy and hard-driving and wailing. It sounded like there were FIVE guitar players in that closet.

I turned to my guys. They were dancing along to the guitar music. Waving their hands high above their heads. Rocking and bopping.

"I… I can't believe it! Chipmunk is *talented*!" Belzer shouted.

"I told you," I said.

"Rotten House is gonna win the contest!"

Crench exclaimed. "No *way* we can lose now!"

I grinned. "Know what, dudes?" I said. "I'm gonna make sure we don't lose."

"Uh-oh," Crench said. "What are you going to do, Bernie?"

My grin grew wider. "I'm going to pay a visit to Nyce House and help Chipmunk out a little."

"You're going into Nyce House?" Feenman asked. "Bernie, you know you start to shake and sweat when you go there."

"Help Chipmunk? What do you mean?" Belzer asked.

I held up a water bottle. "I'm going to sneak into their dorm and water Wes Updood's saxophone," I said. "You know. Fill it up a little."

I pointed to the closet. "A little help for my best buddy Chipmunk, who is going to take me to The Plopps concert."

Crench stared at the water bottle. Then he frowned at me. "But, Bernie – isn't that *cheating?*"

I clapped my hand over Crench's mouth. "Cheating? Don't *ever* say that word," I told him. "It's not cheating. It's *helping!*"

Chapter 14

NOT NICE IN NYCE HOUSE

A bright full moon glowed down on me as I crept across the campus to the Nyce House dorm. I had the water bottle hidden deep in my backpack.

I kept smiling as I pictured Wes Updood stepping onstage tomorrow after school. He raises his golden saxophone to his lips. He starts to play...

And instead of musical notes, we hear *GURGLE GURGLE GURGLE*.

Yes, Bernie B was about to play a very mean trick.

But come on. Isn't *Talent Contest* another word for *WAR*?

I started to shake and sweat as I let myself into Nyce House through the front door. But I didn't care. I was on a mission. A mission to help my buddy Chipmunk.

The front hall was empty. The wood floors gleamed brighter than the moonlight. Sam and Janet Pocketlint must polish them every day.

In Rotten House we've never even *seen* the floor! It's too cluttered with all our junk.

I crept towards the back. I passed three big posters on the wall. In Rotten House we have NASCAR posters in the front hall. And a couple of football posters.

In Nyce House they have posters of *angels* on the wall. Old-fashioned paintings of women floating in the clouds, with big white wings and halos over their heads.

Well, they don't call it *Nyce* House for nothing! I guess Sam and Janet Pocketlint want all their boys to act like angels.

I heard voices in the Commons Room. I stopped at the doorway and peeked in.

Sherman Oaks was in there. And Wes Updood.

And a bunch of other Nyce House guys. Sherman was showing off his drum machine.

"If I push this button I can get a Latin rhythm," Sherman was saying. He pushed a button, and a tango-type beat started up.

"If I push this button it sounds like cymbals crashing," Sherman said. He pushed the button, and cymbals crashed.

"You have to be a *great* musician to push the right buttons," Sherman said.

Yeah. Right.

I was happy. Sherman and Wes were busy here. That meant that Wes's room was empty. That would make it a lot easier to sneak in, fill the sax with water and sneak back out.

Wes's room was just around the corner. I slid the backpack around to the front so I could grab the water bottle.

I was shaking and sweating. My heart started to pound out a Latin rhythm.

I stepped up to Wes's door – and someone grabbed me from behind.

Chapter 15

THE
MUSIC LOVER

I spun round – and stared in horror at Sam and Janet Pocketlint!

"H-h-h-hi!" I stammered. I wanted to faint. But Bernie B never panics. I got it together fast and flashed them my best dimpled smile. "Nice to see you!"

Mr Pocketlint wore his school blazer and tie and baggy, khaki pants. His wife wore a black, pleated dress, down to her ankles.

He has a slender, pink face, a very long, pointed nose and tiny blue eyes, very close together. He looks a lot like one of those anteaters you see in cartoons.

Mrs Pocketlint has grey hair held in place with a headband. Round, grey eyes and a large nose that always seems to be sniffing the air.

"Young man, what are you doing here?" Mr Pocketlint demanded.

I kept the grin on my face. I know no one can resist my adorable dimples. "Well… you see…"

Mrs Pocketlint sniffed the air and squinted at me. "Aren't you Bernie Bridges? We've heard a lot about you."

"Lies! All lies!" I said. "People who are jealous make up lies about me."

"Well, we try to keep the riffraff out of Nyce House. What are you doing here?" Mr Pocketlint asked again.

"Uh… Wes Updood asked me to get his saxophone for him," I said.

They both stared at me. Mr. Pocketlint blinked his tiny, anteater eyes. "Oh, I see," he said. "You're interested in music? Do you like Mozart?"

"I play sonatas on the harpsichord," Mrs Pocketlint said. When she smiled, her pink gums showed. She had two rows of tiny, pointed teeth.

"My left hand is very good," she continued. "But my right hand is only fair."

She smiled her gummy smile at her husband. "Sam plays the ocarina," she said, squeezing his arm.

"Come. Listen to some Mozart," Mr. Pocketlint said. "We heard you were a scheming, fast-talking, troublemaking brat. We didn't know you were a music lover."

"For sure," I said. "I love music. I *live* for music. And of course Mozart is one of my fave's. But if I could just get that saxophone..."

They each grabbed one of my arms. "That can wait," Mrs Pocketlint said. "First Mozart."

"But— but—"

They dragged me into a large room at the end of the hall and locked the door behind me. I saw a grand piano, a harpsichord, two music stands and a couch. The walls had shelves and shelves of old record albums and CDs.

"This is our music room," Mr Pocketlint said. He picked up his ocarina. It looked like a white plastic potato. He pointed with it. "Sit over there."

"But I really need to—"

Mrs Pocketlint sat down at the piano. She sniffed the air and arranged her music in front of her. "Sam and I will start out with some familiar sonatas," she said. "I'm sure you know them."

"Which one is your favourite?" her husband asked.

"Well…" I swallowed. "I guess I like them all," I said.

"Then we'll play them all!" Mrs Pocketlint exclaimed. She lowered her hands and began banging away on the piano. Mr Pocketlint closed his tiny eyes, raised the little flute-thing to his mouth and began to blow.

I settled back on the couch and kept a smile frozen on my face. I tried hard to keep my eyes open, but it was a struggle.

They played for hours and

hours – maybe *days*! I took a short, two-hour nap, but I don't think they noticed.

When they finally finished, they were both red-faced, panting hard and bathed in sweat.

I jumped to my feet. My chance to escape!

"Thank you. Thank you both. That was wonderful!" I said. I clapped them both on the back and shook their hands. "I have tears in my eyes. Tears! Mozart always makes me so emotional!"

Mrs Pocketlint flashed me her gummy smile. "What a delightful young man!"

Mr Pocketlint smiled, too. "We'll invite you back for our eight-hour Brahms festival," he said.

"Only eight hours?" I said. "That isn't enough!"

And I took off, running. I ran down the hall. My ears were ringing from hours of Mozart. And my legs were trembling and weak.

But I still had a mission to accomplish. I still had to sneak into Wes Updood's room and pour water—

Uh-oh.

Where was that music coming from? It sounded like saxophone music.

I followed it to the Commons Room. And there was Wes, head tilted back, on his knees, swinging the sax back and forth as he played.

I failed. Bernie B failed his friend Chipmunk. Head down, I slunk back to the dorm.

Back in Rotten House, I kissed the dirty floor. Feenman and Crench were waiting for me in my room.

"Did you do it, Big B?" Crench asked. "Did you give Wes's saxophone the water treatment?"

"I changed my mind," I said. "We have to win this fair and square."

Feenman felt my forehead. "Fair and square? Are you *sick?*"

"We don't need dirty tricks," I said. "Listen to that awesome guitar music floating up from Chipmunk's closet. He's *awesome!* We can't lose!"

But then, a funny thing happened at the rehearsal...

Chapter 16

WHY I SAT ON CHIPMUNK

The next day, after classes, I hurried to the auditorium in the Student Centre. The rehearsal was just starting. Mrs Twinkler, the Drama teacher, was calling for the first act to come on stage.

"Bright faces, people!" she called. "Bright faces! I want to see everyone glow and shine!"

That's the way she talks. She's very cheery and enthusiastic. She's a real Twinkler.

Kids were scattered all over the auditorium. They had come to watch the auditions.

I hurried backstage to see if Chipmunk was ready.

I saw Flora and Fauna – the Peevish twins – practicing a song near the stage door. Jennifer Ecch waved to me and threw me a kiss. Sherman and Wes and their band were taking their instruments from their cases.

Where was Chipmunk?

Before I could ask anyone, Feenman and Crench came running up to me.

"Where's Chipmunk?" I asked. "The auditions are starting."

"He won't leave his room," Crench said breathlessly. "We tried, Bernie. He said he won't come out."

"He chained himself to the bed," Feenman said. "What should we do?"

"What should you do? *Unchain him!*" I cried. "What's he trying to do? Totally mess me up? How is he going to take me to The Plopps concert if he's chained to his bed?"

"OK, Bernie," Feenman said. "We'll try again, but—"

"Tell him he's a star," I said. "Tell him he's already won. Tell him there's a million dollars for him here. In cash! Tell him *anything*! Just get him here!"

They both saluted and ran off.

I let out a long sigh and dropped into a seat in the front row.

"Glow and shine, people!" Mrs Twinkler bubbled. "Big smiles now. We're *all* stars, remember!"

Jennifer Ecch came on stage first. She sat down on a tall stool. She had a little ventriloquist's dummy in her hands.

"Oh noooo." I let out a loud groan when I saw the dummy clearly. It looked just like *me*!

Jennifer began her ventriloquist act. "This is Bernie," she said. "Say hello, Bernie." She made the dummy say hello in a tiny, squeaky voice. Then she made loud, smoochy noises and had the dummy kiss her back. "Bernie likes to kiss – don't you, Bernie?" she said.

Kids in the auditorium were laughing their heads off. I sank as low in my seat as I could go. Could *anything* be more embarrassing?

Flora and Fauna came on next. "We're going to sing a duet," Flora said. "The song is called 'Getting to Know You'."

"Wonderful!" Mrs Twinkler cried. "Sing it like you feel it!"

The Peevish twins started to sing. They didn't have good voices. They kinda sounded like cows caught in a wire fence. But it went pretty well until Fauna messed up the words.

Her sister stopped singing. "You jerk!" she cried. "You messed it up."

"I didn't mess it up – *you* did!" Fauna screamed.

"You did!"

They started slapping and punching each other. Mrs Twinkler had to drag them off the stage.

"Losers," I muttered to myself. *No way* they can beat Chipmunk.

I glanced to the back of the auditorium. And saw Feenman and Crench dragging Chipmunk down the aisle.

I jumped to my feet. "Here he is! Our star is here! You've already won, dude!"

His whole body was trembling. His teeth chattered and his eyes rolled in his head.

I put a hand on his shaking shoulder. "What's the problem?" I asked.

"I—I—I want my mommy!" Chipmunk said. Then he bit his tongue, so he couldn't say any more.

I turned to Feenman and Crench. "Where's his guitar?"

Feenman slapped his forehead. "Uh-oh. We forgot it."

"GO GET IT!" I screamed. "How do you expect Chipmunk to be a star without his guitar?"

They turned and took off running – again.

Chipmunk tried to run. But I tackled him, held him down on the floor and sat on him. No way he'd escape from Bernie B.

On stage, Wes and his band started to play. Wes leaned way back, raised his sax and sent a beautiful melody floating over the auditorium. Kids started to clap and cheer.

I heard a loud buzz. And saw two white bolts of electricity shoot out of Sherman's drum machine. Sherman let out a shriek – and jumped about two feet in the air.

The drum machine shorted out!

"This will ruin it for these guys," I muttered.

But no. Wes kept right on rocking.

Kids clapped along and shouted even louder than before. And when the band finished, everyone gave them a standing ovation. Mrs Twinkler couldn't get the kids to stop clapping.

"Don't worry about it," I told Chipmunk. "No problem." I was still sitting on him. "They'll forget Wes Updood when you start to play."

Finally, Feenman and Crench came running down the aisle with Chipmunk's guitar. I climbed up and tugged Chipmunk to his feet. I pulled the guitar over his shoulders.

I gave him a shove towards the stage. "Get up

there, dude!" I said. "You rock! You totally rock!"

Chipmunk staggered on to the stage. His legs were shaking so hard, he looked like he was dancing.

I dropped down into my seat between Feenman
and Crench. "We've
got a winner," I said.
"Check him out.
That's what a
winner looks
like!"

Chapter 17

URRRRRRP

"Chipmunk, glow and shine!" Mrs Twinkler said. "A winner has a winning smile!"

Chipmunk couldn't smile. His teeth were chattering too hard.

He raised his guitar. He stared out at the audience.

"Go, dude!" I shouted. "Shake rattle and roll!"

But Chipmunk turned and gazed around. "Where's my closet?" he said.

Mrs Twinkler squinted at him. "Closet?"

"There's no closet," I shouted from the front row. "Just play! Do it, dude! Rock and roll forever!"

Chipmunk's mouth dropped open. "No closet?"

"Go ahead. Never keep an audience waiting," Mrs Twinkler said.

"But— but—" Chipmunk stared down at me. "I can't play unless I'm in a closet!"

"Chipmunk – do it, dude!" I shouted. "Rock the room!"

He glanced around again. "No closet?" He made a loud *urrp*ing sound. "Bernie, help me. I'm going to hurl. Here comes my lunch. I'm going to *hurl!*"

I jumped from my seat. But I couldn't get on stage in time.

Chipmunk bent over his guitar and hurled his guts out.

When he was finished, I helped him off the stage. I turned to Mrs Twinkler and flashed her a big smile. "Just a little stage fright," I said. "He'll be great. You'll see."

Urrrrrrrrrrp.

I guessed wrong. Chipmunk wasn't finished.
I'm doomed! I realised. *DOOMED!*

Chapter 18

URP URP URPURPURP

The next day I ran into April-May June outside the library. She flashed me a teasing grin and her blue eyes sparkled. "Too bad you can't come with Wes and me to The Plopps concert," she said. "But I'll tell the Plopp sisters you said hi when I meet them *in person* backstage."

Why did she enjoy torturing me? Didn't she realise she was my girlfriend?

"Don't get your hopes up, April-May," I said. "Bernie B hasn't given up. I'm still gonna win."

"Ha," she said. "Double ha. How are you going

to win? Chipmunk's big talent is barfing on stage."

"There's a *lot* of other talent in Rotten House," I told her. "I just have to find it."

I hurried to the dorm. I called everyone to a meeting in the Commons Room. I was desperate. I had to find a winning act. The Talent Contest was tomorrow!

I turned to Feenman. "Maybe you, Crench and Belzer can do your *Three Stooges* act. It was funny. It really had me laughing."

"I don't think so!" Feenman backed away. "You want to see my bruises? I'm bandaged in twelve places!"

"I can't *see* straight!" Crench said. "He poked my eyes out!"

"I'm still *bleeding*!" Belzer wailed. "Please – don't make us!"

"Come on, dudes," I said. "What's a little *pain* when the honour of your dorm is at stake?"

But I could see they wouldn't do it. I glanced around the crowd of guys. "Who else has talent? Anybody else?"

A kid from the first floor, named Mason Dixon, pushed his way through the crowd. "I've got talent, Bernie. I can gargle all of Hilary Duff's hit songs."

"Awesome!" I said. "Back up. Give him some room. Let's see what he's got."

Mason filled his mouth with water. He started to gargle. It sounded pretty good – until he choked. He choked for about two minutes and swallowed all the water.

"Next!" I cried. "Who else? Who else?"

To my surprise,

Beast pushed a bunch of guys out of his way and stepped up to me. I took a deep breath. Something stank.

"Beast, have you been chasing skunks again?"

He grinned. "Almost caught one. Almost."

I held my nose. "What's your talent?"

"I can burp the love song from *Star Wars*," he said. "Listen. *Urp urp urpurpurp. Urp urpurp urp—*"

"I don't think so," I said. "Anyone else? Anyone?"

Silence.

"Doomed," I muttered. "Doomed." Shaking my head, I slunk back upstairs to my room.

I was halfway up the stairs when I had an *awesome* idea.

Chapter 19

THE BIG SHOW

The next afternoon, I stepped backstage as the Talent Contest started. Was I nervous? Not at all. I was calm as a carrot.

I peeked out from the side of the curtain. Every seat in the auditorium was filled. Every kid in school had turned out to watch my victory.

Mrs Twinkler called Flora and Fauna Peevish to perform first. "Glow and shine, girls! Glow and shine!"

But they didn't glow and shine. Flora started singing while Fauna was still clearing her throat. So they had to start again. Then Fauna messed up the words.

The two sisters started slapping and hitting each other, and Mrs Twinkler had to drag them off the stage again.

The kids in the audience were *not* polite. They booed and hissed, and someone tossed a shoe on the stage.

Someone tapped me on the shoulder. I turned to see Feenman and Crench with big grins on their faces. "Hey dudes," I said, "how's it going?"

Then I saw that Feenman had a power drill in his hand. "What's up with that?" I asked.

He raised a finger to his lips. "Ssshhh. Bernie," he whispered, "we just drilled a few *extra holes* in Wes Updood's saxophone. He won't notice till he starts to play."

They both giggled.

"Good work," I said. "Wes and his band are up next."

"Where's Chipmunk?" Crench asked.

I pointed behind us. "I've got two guys sitting on him backstage so he won't run

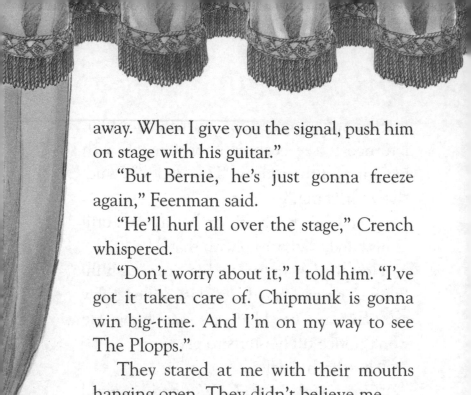

away. When I give you the signal, push him on stage with his guitar."

"But Bernie, he's just gonna freeze again," Feenman said.

"He'll hurl all over the stage," Crench whispered.

"Don't worry about it," I told him. "I've got it taken care of. Chipmunk is gonna win big-time. And I'm on my way to see The Plopps."

They stared at me with their mouths hanging open. They didn't believe me.

Wes, Sherman and the Nyce House Band were setting up on stage.

"These cats are really cool!" Mrs Twinkler was announcing. "They really

swing. They're going to rock your world!"

Feenman giggled. "Wait till Wes discovers the extra holes in his sax! That'll rock *his* world!"

Crench giggled, too. "He'll blow so hard his head will explode!"

Sherman pushed a button and started his drumbeats.

Wes stepped to the edge of the stage. "Fried rice, everyone!" he shouted. "Angel hair pasta! Downtown. Downtown!"

So cool.

He took a few steps back and started to play. The band started slowly, picked up steam, then totally rocked.

Watching from the side of the stage, I had to admit it: Wes was *awesome*!

And the extra holes in his sax gave him NEW HIGH NOTES! He wailed and trilled the new notes till everyone was *screaming*! They jumped up and danced and rocked to the music. And when it ended they screamed and stamped their feet for more.

Mrs Twinkler couldn't get them to stop.

I turned and saw Feenman and Crench shaking their heads sadly. "Sorry Bernie,"

Crench said. "We tried. We really did. Better luck next year."

"Are you kidding?" I said. "We're gonna win. Trust me. It's all over. We win!" I pointed to the back. "Hurry. Go get Chipmunk. Strap on his guitar and shove him out there."

Was I nervous now?

You're joking, right?

Calm as a carrot.

I was already daydreaming about what I'd say to the Plopp sisters when I met them…

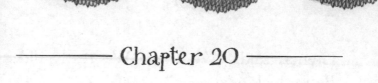

— Chapter 20 —

WE HAVE A WINNER AND A LOSER!

Chipmunk looked a little dazed. His eyes bulged and his lips were trembling.

We strapped his guitar on, and all three of us pushed him on stage. His legs were shaking so

hard we actually had to carry him.

"Chipmunk is going to favour us with some guitar stylings!" Mrs Twinkler told the audience. She smiled at Chipmunk. "Glow and shine now. And don't barf!"

Chipmunk gazed out at the huge crowd of kids. I don't think he heard Mrs Twinkler. His whole body began to shake and shudder.

The kids thought it was part of the act. They started to clap along.

He turned all around. "Wh-where's my c-closet?" he stammered. "Bernie? My closet?" His eyes suddenly shut. "Uh-oh. I'm going to *hurl*. Where's my closet?"

"HERE'S YOUR CLOSET!" I shouted. I pushed it out on stage.

Chipmunk blinked. "My closet?"

"Here it is," I said. "I tore it out of your wall."

Hey – Bernie B will do *anything* for his guys!

I never saw Chipmunk look so happy. He leaped into the closet and I slammed the door shut.

I turned to the audience. "Here he is, everyone! The Hidden Guitarist!"

After a few seconds Chipmunk began to twang and rock. Do I have to tell you

what happened next?

His guitar playing was so totally *beyond* awesome, the audience wouldn't let him stop. Every time he ended a song, the audience screamed for more.

The kids were standing on their seats, dancing everywhere, doing cartwheels down the aisle.

Too bad Chipmunk couldn't see it!

He rocked for an hour. And after he stopped, the kids screamed for at least *another* hour!

It took the judges less than ten seconds to decide. CHIPMUNK was the WINNER!

"You did it, Big B! You did it!" Feenman

and Crench shouted, jumping up and down, pumping their fists in the air.

"For sure!" I said. We slapped high fives and low fives, touched knuckles and did the secret Rotten School Handshake.

I looked around the stage. "Hey – where's Chipmunk?"

Feenman slapped his forehead. "We left him in the closet!"

We ran across the stage, tugged open the closet door and pulled Chipmunk out. "Air! Air!" he gasped. His face was blue, but after a few seconds it returned to the right color.

"Chipmunk, buddy! You won! You won!"
I told him, slapping him on the back.

His eyes grew wide. "I did? I won? Oh,
wow." He blushed. "I couldn't have done it
without you."

April-May came running up to us, her
blond hair flying. "Chipmunk –
congratulations!" she cried "You're going
to The Plopps concert!
Congratulations!"

Chipmunk blushed.
He grinned at April-May.

"Would you like to go with me?" he asked.

"Yes!" she cried. "I'm there! I'm there! Yes!"

Chipmunk turned to me. "See, Bernie? You're helping me get over my shyness!"

I couldn't breathe. I couldn't talk. Chipmunk and April-May walked off, talking excitedly about the concert.

April-May?

He's taking April-May?

"Hey, Bernie," Feenman called after me. "Hey, wait – Bernie. Where are you going?"

"Where do you think?" I said.

I climbed into the closet and slammed the door.

HERE'S A SNEAK PEEK AT BOOK 6 IN

R.L. STINE'S

ROTTEN SCHOOL

The Heinie Prize

WHY THE TWINS SCREAMED

I hurried to the girls' dorm to find Flora Peevish and her twin sister, Fauna. They hang out a lot with Sherman Oaks, but I didn't care about that tonight. I was desperate.

I found them in their dorm's Commons Room watching Japanese sumo wrestling on TV with a bunch of other girls. The girls were all jumping up and down on the couches, cheering and shouting.

One of them gave me a nice greeting: "Beat it!"

I pointed to the huge dudes in diapers wrestling on TV. "How can you watch those guys?" I asked.

"We think they're cute," she answered.

"Awesome," I said. "You know Belzer, right? You think he's cute too?"

She stuck her finger down her throat and gagged herself.

"Is that a yes or a no?" I asked.

"Ucccck," her sister said.

I turned to Fauna. "Be honest. What do you think of Belzer?" I asked.

She groaned. "He's like a piece of something you pull out from between your toes."

"So you have a crush on him?" I said.

"Uccccck."

On TV, the diaper dudes were falling on each other. The girls cheered and shrieked.

I pulled the Peevish twins into the hall. "Look. I need your help," I said. "I'm doing a science experiment. For extra credit in Mr Boring's class."

"What's the experiment?" Fauna asked.

"I need you to pretend to have *major* crushes on Belzer," I said.

"I'd rather eat cow plop," Flora said.

"Sign me up for that," Fauna said.

I laughed. "Ha-ha-ha. Belzer *loves* girls with a sense of humour!"

"I'm not joking," Flora said. "Bring me the cow plop. I'll show you."

"It's just *pretend*," I said. "Just *pretend* you both have a crush on him. It's an experiment. To build up his confidence. To see if it'll make him change."

"No way," Fauna said, turning up her already-turned-up nose. "Not even pretend."

"I sat next to Belzer at the movies," Flora said, "and he picked his nose the entire time."

"I could hear his stomach growling," Fauna said. "It sounded like he had a cat trapped in there. He burped up some of his lunch and then he *ate* it."

"How about if I bribe you?" I asked.

They stared at me. "What's the bribe?"

"Two six-packs of Foamy Root Beer," I said.

Their eyes lit up. "Two six-packs?" Fauna asked.

I knew they don't drink it. They use it for shampoo because it's so foamy.

"OK. What do we have to do?" Flora asked.

"Follow me," I said. "Belzer is in the laundry room. Just go in there and make a big fuss over the guy."

"How long do we have to flirt with him?" Fauna asked.

"Give him fifteen minutes. Can you do it?" I asked.

"Ten minutes," Fauna said.

We settled on twelve.

We followed the path across the Great Lawn to the Student Centre.

I knew this would help Belzer a lot. Help build his confidence. And I'd make sure to get word to Mrs Heinie about how popular Belzer was with the girls – because he was so *outstanding*.

The twins followed me through the back door and down the steps to the laundry room. We walked into the bright lights.

And then all three of us gasped. Flora and Fauna opened their mouths – and let out deafening SCREAMS.

Belzer stood there TOTALLY NAKED.

"Belzer? What are you DOING?" I cried.

He shrugged. "Bernie, you told me to wash ALL my clothes!"

ABOUT THE AUTHOR

R.L. Stine graduated from the Rotten School with a solid D+ average, which put him at the top of his class. He says that his favourite activities at school were Scratching Body Parts and Making Armpit Noises.

In sixth grade, R.L. won the school Athletic Award for his performance in the Wedgie Championships. Unfortunately, after the tournament, his underpants had to be surgically removed.

After graduation, R.L. became well known for writing scary book series such as *The Nightmare Room*, *Fear Street*, *Goosebumps*, and *Mostly Ghostly*, and a short story collection called *Beware!*

Today, R.L. lives in New York City, where he is busy writing stories about his school days.

For more information about R.L. Stine, go to www.rottenschool.com and www.rlstine.com